CORDUROY'S
Best Halloween Ever!

Grosset & Dunlap

A bear's share of the royalties from the sale of
Corduroy's Best Halloween Ever! goes to the Don and
Lydia Freeman Research Fund to support
psychological care and research concerning
children with life-threatening illness.

Some material in this book was first published in *Corduroy's Halloween* in 1995 by Viking,
a division of Penguin Putnam Inc.

Library of Congress Cataloging-in-Publication Data is available.

ISBN 978-0-448-42499-6   27 29 30 28

Corduroy's Best Halloween Ever!

BASED ON THE CHARACTER CREATED BY DON FREEMAN

ILLUSTRATED BY LISA McCUE

Grosset & Dunlap, Publishers

It was almost Halloween! Corduroy and his friends were getting ready. They went to pick out a pumpkin for Corduroy's Halloween party.

There was so much to do before the party.
Corduroy raked the leaves. Rabbit, Puppy, and
Mouse tried to help, but jumping in the leaf piles
was much more fun!

Corduroy and his friends helped Mrs. Pig
decorate her store windows. She thanked
them with a hot, delicious pumpkin pie. Yum!

Back at Corduroy's house, they all started talking about their costumes for Halloween.

"I'm going to be a pumpkin!" said Mouse.

"I'm going as a lion!" said Rabbit. "The king of the jungle!"

"My costume is a secret," said Puppy. "It's really great. I want you all to be surprised."

Corduroy was worried. He didn't have an idea for a costume yet. What would he wear for Halloween?

?

Later, while Corduroy was shopping for his party,
he spotted a whole bunch of costumes. Finding a
costume would be easy with all of these choices.

PUMPKIN

COSTUME

MCCUE

Corduroy tried on the lion costume. Roar! He looked ferocious. But then he remembered that Rabbit was dressing up as a lion.

He tried on the pumpkin costume. It fit perfectly! But oops—didn't Mouse say he was going as a pumpkin?

I know, thought Corduroy, I will be a scary witch with a pointy hat. But then he remembered something. His friend Dolly wanted to dress up as a witch.

Then he saw the perfect thing. A dinosaur mask! Wow, thought Corduroy. I can make a great costume to go with that mask!

Corduroy went home to work on his costume.
He found an old pair of green pajamas and some
scraps of fabric.

He cut. He glued. He even sewed.

Finally, he was finished.

Halloween night finally came. Corduroy was so excited for his party. *Ding-dong!* The doorbell rang! Who could it be? The party wasn't supposed to start for another hour.

Corduroy opened the door. Puppy looked very sad.
"Corduroy, I had the best costume, and it fell apart!
It's all in pieces. What should I do?"

Corduroy thought about it. He loved his costume. But
Puppy was so sad. And Corduroy knew that friends were
more important than costumes.

"It's okay, Puppy. I have a costume you can wear!"

"Really?" said Puppy. "But Corduroy, what will you wear?"
"Don't worry, I have an idea," said Corduroy. But he didn't, really. What *would* he wear?

Corduroy thought and thought. He thought all through the party. It was a really fun party, too! They bobbed for apples and carved jack-o'-lanterns and ate cookies and punch.

They even danced the Monster Mash!
It was almost time to go trick-or-treating.
And Corduroy still didn't have a costume.

Suddenly, he really did have an idea. He carefully moved everything off of the table. He held up the tablecloth. Perfect! thought Corduroy.

He cut holes for eyes and a mouth. He looked at the punch and chocolate stains all over the tablecloth.

"I am a ghost who just came from
a Halloween party!" said Corduroy.
All his friends laughed. It *was* a great costume.
"Let's go trick-or-treat!"

Everybody loved Corduroy's costume.
"What a creative idea!" they said.

Corduroy felt proud.
And Puppy loved his
dinosaur costume.
Everyone was happy!

It was the best Halloween ever!